Sophie
Hits Six

First published 1991 by Walker Books Ltd
87 Vauxhall Walk, London SE11 5HJ

This edition published 2000

2 4 6 8 10 9 7 5 3 1

Text © 1991 Fox Busters Ltd
Illustrations © 1991 David Parkins
Cover illustrations © 1991, 1999 David Parkins

The right of Dick King-Smith and David Parkins to be identified as
author and illustrator respectively of this work has been asserted by them
in accordance with the Copyright, Designs and Patents Act 1988

This book has been typeset in Giovanni

Printed and bound in Italy by ▓▓ Grafica Veneta S.p.A.

British Library Cataloguing in Publication Data:
a catalogue record for this book is available from the British Library

ISBN 978-0-7445-7721-1

www.walker.co.uk

Sophie
Hits Six

Dick King-Smith

illustrated by
David Parkins

**WALKER
BOOKS**

Contents

Tomboy

"One thing's certain," said Sophie's father. "You can't call him … her … Tom any more."

Tom was Sophie's black cat, who had come from nowhere and adopted her, and had now, much to everyone's surprise, given birth to four kittens.

"Female cats are called queens," said Sophie's mother. "You could call her Queenie."

"I don't like that," said Sophie.

"How about Elizabeth?" said Matthew, who was eight, two and a half years older than Sophie and

ten minutes older than his twin brother Mark.

"Why Elizabeth?"

"Well, it's the Queen's name."

"Or Anne?" said Mark.

'"Why?"

"That's what the Queen's daughter is called."

The twins were quite taken with this idea of royalty. As often happened, they had the same thought at the same moment, and they looked at one another and grinned and said, "How about Fergie?"

"Spelt F-U-R-gie," said Sophie's father, and everyone laughed, except Sophie.

"You're all mowldy, stupid and assive!" she said, and she stumped off, hands rammed deep into the pockets of her old jeans, a frown of disapproval on her round face.

She plodded
up to the attic
at the top of
the house,
where all the
animals of
her toy farm
were laid out.
Here, in the depths of
an old armchair, lay her
cat, nursing the four kittens,
one tabby, one tortoiseshell,
one black with a white bib and white
feet and one exactly like its mother, whose
black coat Sophie now stroked.

"I can't call you Tom any more," she said,
"because you're not one, are you, my dear?"

"Nee-o," said the cat, or that's how it sounded
to Sophie.

"I suppose I could call you Thomasina, but
I don't much fancy that, do you?"

"Nee-o."

"Mum and Daddy and the twins weren't any help."

Sophie rubbed the tip of her nose, a sure sign
that she was thinking deeply.

"I wish Aunt Al was here," she said. "I bet she'd
have a good idea."

Aunt Al was Sophie's father's great-aunt, and
therefore Sophie's great-great-aunt. When she had
first been told this, she had imagined Aunt Al as
enormous, but actually she was very small, with
thin legs like a bird. She was nearly eighty-two years
old, and she lived in the Highlands of Scotland.
She and Sophie had become great friends.

Sophie sat on the arm of the old chair, stroking her nameless cat and wondering whether to write a letter to Aunt Al.

"Trouble is," she said, "I'd have to have help with the spelling and everything, and anyway it would all take a long time."

Just then she heard the trill of the telephone downstairs, and she jumped up, grinning.

"Yikes!" said Sophie. "That's it! I'll ring her!"

Something told Sophie it might be best to say nothing to the others about this phone call. It could perhaps be rather expensive to telephone the Highlands because they were so high. If they ask me, she thought, I'll tell them I did it (for Sophie disapproved of lying), but if they don't know, they won't ask.

So she waited that afternoon, a fine Saturday

afternoon in early May,
until her brothers had
gone off to play football
(of which they never
tired) with some
friends, her mother
had gone to do
some shopping
and her father
was working in
the garden.

Sophie found Aunt Al's
number in the phone book and carefully dialled it.
She heard the ringing tone, and then Aunt Al's
brisk voice, as loud and clear as if she were in the
room, saying, "Hello. Who is it?"

"It's Sophie."

"Sophie? My niece?"

"Great-great-niece, Aunt Al."

"Great-great-aunt to you. How nice to hear your voice, Sophie. Are you OK? Anything the matter?"

"Yes, there is."

"Nobody ill or anything?"

"No. It's my cat."

"Tom?"

"Yes. Well, no. You see, it's not Tom any more, because she's had four babies."

"Whew!" said Aunt Al. "Surprise, surprise."

"And so she's got to have a new name," said Sophie, "and I can't think of a good one. That's why I'm ringing you up, to ask if you can help me."

"Right," said Aunt Al. "Give me a minute."

Sophie waited, imagining, as she always did, Aunt Al sitting on top of a mountain somewhere,

14

surrounded by golden eagles and blue hares and red deer. In a minute her voice would come whizzing down the telephone wires, down the mountainside, off the edge of the Highlands, out of Scotland, and all the way nearly to the bottom of England, all in a fraction of a second.

"Tomboy," said Aunt Al.

"What?" said Sophie. "That's even worse than plain Tom."

"No, it's not. Don't you know what a tomboy is?"

"No."

"A tomboy is a high-spirited girl that likes romping about. Your cat's high-spirited, isn't she?"

"Yes."

"Well then."

One of the reasons why Sophie and Aunt Al got on so well was they were both direct, no-nonsense

people. They did what had to be done, said
what had to be said, and that was the end of it.

"OK," said Sophie. "Thanks. See you."

"Sometime in the summer, I hope," said
Aunt Al, and rang off.

At tea-time Sophie said, "My cat's got her new
name."

"What is it?" chorused the twins.

"Tomboy."

"What?" they said. "That's even worse than
plain Tom."

"Don't they teach you anything in your class?"
said Sophie scornfully. "You're ingerant, that's
what you are."

"Don't you mean 'ignorant'?" said her father.

"That too," said Sophie.

"But Sophie," said
her mother, "do you know
what 'tomboy' means?"

"Of course," said Sophie. "A tomboy is a high-spirited girl that likes romping about. Can I get down please?"

"Yes," said her mother, "if you've finished. Where are you off to?"

"To feed Tomboy," said Sophie, "and to find names for my four kittens." And off she plodded.

Sophie, though small, was very determined, and a worrying thought crossed her mother's mind.

"I do hope," she said, "she doesn't think that she can keep those kittens."

"One thing's certain," said Sophie's father, "she can't. As soon as they're old enough, we must find them homes. One cat's enough, let alone five."

Up in the attic, Sophie addressed the kittens. Her firm ambition in life was to be a lady farmer, and she knew well that farmers, whether ladies or

no, were always looking to increase their flocks
and herds.

"Now, my dears," she said, "let's hope that you're
all girls. Then, once you're big enough, you can all
have babies too. And suppose each of you has four,
that will make … let's see –" and Sophie began to
count upon her fingers.

Down On The Farm

Sophie liked school. Learning things, she had decided by the end of her first term, was interesting, even though they did not have Farming Lessons, as she had hoped they would. But she could see that to be a lady farmer one day meant that you had to know how to read and write and do sums, so she set about these tasks in her usual determined manner.

Early in the summer term, her teacher was asked

by the headmistress, "How is Sophie getting on?"

"Very well really. She takes a lot of trouble with her work. Wants to be a farmer, she tells me, so we do a lot of number work with the bottles of milk in the morning! Strange little girl though – lives in a world of her own."

"Still a bit of a loner, is she?"

"A bit. She certainly doesn't have a special friend in the class."

"Who's your special friend, Sophie?" her mother said one evening.

"Tomboy," said Sophie.

"No, I mean at school. In your class."

"Dawn?" said Matthew.

Dawn was a pretty little fair-haired girl, always beautifully dressed, the exact opposite of Sophie, both in looks and nature.

"Yuk!" said Sophie.

"Duncan?" said Mark.

Duncan was a very small, fat, short-legged boy with ginger hair. A one-time playmate of Sophie's, he had been "stolen" by Dawn while Sophie was away having chicken-pox. Both had paid dearly for this.

"He's a wally," said Sophie.

"Don't you like any of the children in your class then, Sophie?" asked her father.

"Not specially. Andrew's all right."

Her mother waited until Sophie had plodded off upstairs to play with the kittens, and then she said to the twins, "Who's Andrew?"

"He's new this term," said Mark.

"He's a farmer's son," said Matthew.

"Aha! Is he nice?"

"Dunno," they said. "We don't play with the infants."

In point of fact Sophie hadn't decided whether Andrew was nice or not – nor did she care. Once she had found out that his father was a farmer, she had determined to make a friend of him. Then, she thought, he would invite her to tea at the farm, and after a bit she would be able to go there often. She would be so useful to Andrew's father that he would ask her to come and help regularly – every day perhaps. And when she left school, she could work there. And, later, she and Andrew would probably get married and have four babies, just like Tomboy, and live happily ever after on the farm.

With such a prospect in view, what did it matter whether she liked Andrew or not?

Sophie took her time. She did not try to bribe him with sweets, as Dawn would have done, nor did she set out to boss him as she had bossed Duncan. Instead she began to ask Andrew lots of questions – about farming of course – whenever she just happened to find herself standing next to him in the playground.

Sophie's reason for this questioning was purely and simply to learn things that would be useful to her one day.

Andrew however, a sturdy little boy of about Sophie's height and build, but with very fair, almost white, hair, was flattered to be thought so knowledgeable, and answered these queries readily, if not always accurately.

"Your dad's a farmer, isn't he?" was Sophie's first question.

"Yes," said Andrew.

"I'm going to be a farmer
when I grow up."

"You can't."

"Why not?"

"Farmers are men."

"Well," said Sophie, "I'm going
to be a lady farmer. So there."

"I'm going to be a man farmer."

"You're lucky," said Sophie, "living on a farm now.
Has your dad got cows?"

"Yes, hundreds."

"Can you milk them?"

"Yes, course I can."

"What else can you do?"

"Drive a tractor," said Andrew. He gripped an
imaginary steering-wheel, engaged an imaginary

gear, and set off round the playground shouting,
"Broom-a-broom-a-broom-a-broom!"

Sophie stood waiting until he had completed
a circuit, pulled on an imaginary handbrake and
switched off.

"I wish I could see your tractor," she said.

But instead of the hoped-for
invitation, Andrew only said,
"It's green."

"How much did it cost?"

"'Bout half a million pounds."

"Yikes!" said Sophie.
"Your dad must
be rich!"

"He is," said Andrew.
"And I shall be too
when I grow up.

I shall have six tractors and I shall have cows and pigs and sheep and chickens and ducks and geese and …"

"… a Shetland pony?" said Sophie.

"Lots of them."

Each day now, at morning and afternoon playtimes, Sophie plied Andrew with questions of an agricultural nature. The fact that she monopolized his company did not escape the notice of her brothers.

Matthew and Mark prided themselves on being fast runners and, with the school's summer sports in mind, spent their time in highspeed dashes across the playground – in which, not surprisingly, they almost always deadheated. However, they could not help but see that each time they hurled themselves against the chain-link fence that acted as a finishing line, there were Sophie and Andrew, dark and fair heads together, chattering away nineteen to the dozen.

"Sophie's always talking to that Andrew," they said to their parents.

"Why ever shouldn't she?" said their mother. "It's nice she's made a special friend at last, and he's a nice-looking little boy too."

"He's not my special friend," said Sophie. "He just knows all about farming, that's all."

"Must be a clever chap," said her father. "How old is he?"

"Five."

"Fancy!"

"Sophie fancies Andrew!" chanted the twins, and they ran off before Sophie had time to tell them that not only were they mowldy, but also both stupid and assive.

"Don't take any notice, darling," said her mother. "They're only teasing."

"It doesn't worry me," said Sophie loftily. "They only do it to be iterating."

"Don't you mean 'irritating'?" said her father.

"Both," said Sophie.

A couple of weeks went by, during which time Sophie continued her questioning. She was also made to move her own livestock from the attic to the potting-shed at the bottom of the garden.

"I'm not having those kittens messing all over the attic," her mother said.

"But they'll mess all over the potting-shed," said Sophie.

"And you'll clear it all up. That's what farmers spend most of their time doing, you know – clearing up all the muck their animals make."

"Your cows must make an awful lot of cowpats," Sophie said to Andrew the next day. "I wish I could see them."

"See the cowpats?"

"No, the cows."

"You can if you like."

"You'll have to ask me to tea."

"All right."

Sophie sighed. Silly boy, she thought, I'll have to fix it all myself, I can see.

"You ask your mummy to ask my mummy if I can," she said, "and then she can bring me."

"All right."

So at the end of the school day Andrew's mother
saw her son approaching, his hand firmly held
by a stocky little girl with an untidy mop of dark

hair and a determined expression. Sophie's mother arrived in time to hear the ensuing conversation.

"Go on, Andrew, ask her," said Sophie.

"Mum," said Andrew. "Can Sophie come to tea?"

"She'd obviously fixed the whole thing up herself," Sophie's mother said to her husband. "I'd never even met the boy's mother before, but she seemed very nice. I said we'd pick Sophie up again about six."

"She'll have got herself into a lovely mess, I shouldn't wonder."

"Oh, I don't know – I made her take her wellies."

The phone rang in the hall.

Sophie's mother came back from answering it.

"You were right," she said. "That was Andrew's mother saying could I bring some clean clothes,

Sophie is absolutely filthy. She slipped up and sat down in a really squelchy cowpat."

"Ah well," said Sophie's father. "Farming's just like any other job. Start at the bottom and work up."

Beano

Down in the potting-shed the four kittens were growing fast. Though Sophie kept the door shut while she was at school (for fear that a Fierce Cat-eating Dog should jump into the garden and gobble them all up), there was a small hole in the boards at the back of the shed, through which Tomboy came and went at her pleasure.

Sophie liked choosing names, and, confident that the kittens were all female, had decided after much thought to call them Molly, Dolly, Holly and Polly.

"Those are all girls' names," her father said.

"They're all girls," said Sophie.

"How d'you know?"

"I just do."

"Wouldn't it be better to give them names that sound different?" her mother asked. "Those all sound the same."

"It's easy to tell them apart," Sophie said. "Molly's the tabby, Dolly's the tortoiseshell, Holly's the black-and-white one and Polly's all black."

Her mother sighed. "That's not quite what I meant," she said.

"It makes no odds," said Sophie's father. "In a couple of weeks they'll all have to go, Sophie. I hope you realize that?"

"Can't I even keep one?"

"No."

* * *

"It's not fair," said Sophie to the twins. "They won't let me keep any of the kittens."

"You've got Tomboy," said Matthew.

"You don't want five cats," said Mark.

"I do," said Sophie. "While I'm waiting to be a lady farmer I could be a lady cat-breeder. If I could keep Molly and Dolly and Holly and Polly and they all had babies, I could sell loads of kittens and save up loads of money for my farm." And she pointed at her piggy-bank, on whose side was stuck a notice which read:

Farm munny
thank you
Sophie

"They won't let you," said the twins.

*   *   *

Two weeks went by, and Sophie's father placed an advertisement in the local paper.

"Four pretty kittens," it said. "Good homes wanted."

"I wouldn't mind, if only you were boys," said Sophie as she sat on the floor of the potting-shed while the kittens played around her. "But it's such a waste. Female animals are much the most important – any farmer knows that."

Just then she heard voices, and in a moment her mother appeared in the doorway with a tall lady.

"Ah," she said. "Here's Sophie, with her kittens. Now, was it a boy you wanted, or a girl?"

"A queen," said the large tall lady. "A female."

"These are all female, Sophie says. Can you tell?"

"Of course," said the large tall lady. "Kept cats all

my life. One
of these is
certainly a
little queen,
I can tell you
that straight
off," and she
pointed at
Dolly.

"How do
you know?" said
Sophie's mother.

"Tortoiseshell. Torts are always
female. Let's have a look at the other
three ... let's see now ... you're a boy ... and
you're a boy ... and you're a boy. Three little toms."

"Oh," said Sophie glumly.

"So I'll take the little tortoiseshell if I may. Does she have a name?"

"Dolly," said Sophie gloomily.

"And you're Sophie?"

Sophie nodded. Only one female, she thought, and she has to go and pick that one.

"So how much do you want for Dolly, Sophie?" asked the large tall lady.

"Excuse me," said Sophie's mother. "I can hear the phone ringing. I shan't be a minute," and out she went.

Sophie rubbed the tip of her nose. I'll say a silly price, she thought, and then she'll say, "Oh, that's much too much," and then she won't take Dolly.

"Five pounds," she said.

The large tall lady produced her purse, and from it she took a five-pound note.

"That's fair enough," she said. "I don't believe in getting something for nothing," and she handed Sophie the money.

"And when the woman had gone off with the kitten," Sophie's mother said to her husband that evening, "I went down to the potting-shed to comfort Sophie, and, lo and behold, she'd flogged it for a fiver."

"'Farm munny'!" said Sophie's father admiringly. "And still three to go!"

However, Sophie was to find that other people were not so generous.

In the days that followed, the black-and-white kitten went to an old man who gave Sophie twenty pence ("For your piggy-bank, young lady"), and the tabby to a jolly couple who gave Sophie a nice

smile and
a pat on
the head.

Now only
the black
kitten remained.

"I wonder where you will go, my dear?" said
Sophie sadly. Soon there would be no kittens
to play with.

"You'll miss them, won't you?" said Sophie
to Tomboy.

"Nee-o."

Just then Sophie heard her mother calling.

"Hurry!" she cried. "It's Aunt Al on the phone. She wants to talk to you."

Sophie galloped up the lawn.

"Hello, Aunt Al," she said breathlessly.

"You sound puffed."

"I was running."

"Tomboy's kittens. Have they all gone?"

"All but one."

"Keep it for me."

"For you?"

"Yes. My old cat's died. He was very ancient, miles older than me if you multiply by seven like you do with a dog's age. Daddy's coming up to Scotland on business next month and bringing me back to stay. D'you think you could keep your last kitten another four weeks, till I can collect it?"

"Oh yes!"

"What colour is it?"

"Black, like Tomboy."

"Lucky," said Aunt Al.

"If they come to you from the right-hand side."

"What's it called?"

"Polly."

"So it's female?"

"No, actually. I thought she was but he isn't."

"We'll have to change the name. So he gets used to a new one before I come."

"You choose then," said Sophie.

"Right," said Aunt Al. "Give me a minute."

Sophie waited, thinking of Aunt Al on her mountain and feeling very glad that the black kitten would live happily at the top of the Highlands.

"Are you still there?" said Aunt Al.

"Yes."

"Ollie. Short for Oliver."

"OK."

"How much d'you want for him?"

"Nothing."

"We'll see about that."

They sounded equally determined.

"Let me speak to your mother."

"OK," said Sophie. "Here she is. See you," and she plodded off down to the potting-shed to tell the good news to Tomboy and Ollie.

Meanwhile her mother was saying on the telephone, "In exchange for the kitten, you mean? What a nice idea, Aunt Al – you know how mad about animals she is ... no, her father won't object, I'll make sure of that ... yes, we'll see about somewhere to keep it … no, we'll keep it a secret, shan't say a word – you can spring the surprise when you come."

When Aunt Al did come, four weeks later, the very first thing she wanted to do was to see Ollie. And Sophie made sure that he came to her from the right-hand side.

"He's beautiful," said Aunt Al, picking the kitten up, while Tomboy wrapped herself around the old lady's thin bird's legs and made her steam-engine noise. "He's the spitting image of his mother. You'll miss him, won't you, Tomboy?"

"Nee-o."

"It's very nice of you to give him to me, Sophie," said Aunt Al. "Maybe I can give you something in return, one of these days."

* * *

Little did Sophie know, when she went to bed that night, what was covered over with an old sheet at the back of the garage.

Little did she guess, when she woke the next morning, what would be put in the potting-shed while she was at school, and while her great-great-aunt was paying a visit to the local pet-shop.

Little did she dream that, when she came home that afternoon, Aunt Al would suggest a walk down to the potting-shed and then, before they went in, would say to her, "Shut your eyes, Sophie."

"Why?"

"Surprise."

Sophie shut her eyes and felt her hand held by another that was skinny and bony and curled like a bird's claws.

"OK," said Aunt Al. "You can look now."

There, sitting placidly in a large new rabbit-hutch, was a large new rabbit. A white rabbit with floppy ears and pink eyes and a wiffly nose.

"Yours," said Aunt Al.

"Yikes!" said Sophie.

Slow and Steady Wins the Race

Sophie hit upon a name for her rabbit quite simply.

"Why has he got pink eyes?" she asked Aunt Al.

"Because he's albino."

Al Beano, thought Sophie. Funny name, but if you take off the Al – after all, we've got one of those in the family – that just leaves Beano. I like that.

At first, Sophie was worried about Tomboy. What would she think of Beano? Cats killed little wild rabbits, she felt sure. What about big tame ones? She found out the answer very soon after Beano's arrival, when he was hopping about the floor and Tomboy suddenly came in through the hole in the back of the shed. Sophie had looked round to see the black cat creeping forward, tail lashing.

But before she could move, the big white rabbit first gave an almighty thump on the floor with his hind legs and then, with a kind of a growl, made a dash at Tomboy, who turned and fled.

Matthew and Mark did not share Sophie's feeling for animals. They were polite to Tomboy and to the new rabbit, but what they were mad about was sport. Their ambition was to play professional football (in the same team, of course, and in the Premier League, naturally) when they were grown-up.

The highlight of the summer term for them was the school sports day. Fast runners both, they were set on beating all the other boys of their age when the great day came.

Sophie was not a fast runner.

"But I would like to win something," she said to

Beano as he lolloped around the floor of the
potting-shed, while she cleaned out his hutch.

Sophie strewed fresh sawdust on the floor of the
hutch, and filled the hayrack, the feeding dish and
the water-bottle. "There you are, my dear," she said.
"All nice and tidy. In you go, there's a good boy."

She used this last word with confidence.
Admittedly, she'd been slightly wrong about Tom,
and later about Molly, Holly and Polly, but Aunt Al
had assured her that the pet-shop owner had
assured *her* that the rabbit was definitely a buck.

She latched the door of the hutch and went to
find her brothers.

They were practising baton-changing on the lawn,
preparing for the lower junior boys' relay race.

"When it's sports day," she said to them, "what
could I win?"

"How fast are you?" they said.

"Not very," said Sophie.

"Let's see," said Matthew.

"We'll give you a good start," said Mark.

"From the path here …"

"…to the other end of the lawn."

"Ready?" said Matthew.

"Steady?" said Mark.

"Go!" they shouted.

Sophie plodded off at her best speed, shoulders hunched, arms pumping, a look of grim determination on her face, and when she was half-way across, the boys gave chase. They flashed past and stood waiting for her at the other end.

"You're not," said Mark.

"Not what?"

"Very fast," said Matthew.

They looked at one another thoughtfully.

"I know!" said Mark.

"I know what you're going to say!" said Matthew.

"The infants' three-legged race!" they cried.

"What's that?"

"Well, you have a partner ..."

"... and you stand next to him ..."

"... with your inside legs tied together ..."

"...so there's two legs on the outside and one in the middle."

"We'll show you," they said, and they ran off and came back with a piece of old rope.

Sophie watched them. They seemed to go almost as fast when bound together, as separately, so well balanced were they.

"You want to pick someone exactly your size," said Matthew.

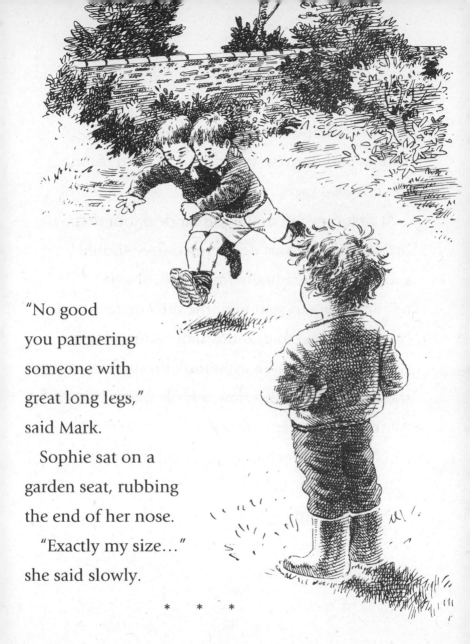

"No good
you partnering
someone with
great long legs,"
said Mark.

Sophie sat on a
garden seat, rubbing
the end of her nose.

"Exactly my size..."
she said slowly.

*   *   *

So it was, that every playtime from then on Sophie and Andrew solemnly practised for the three-legged race.

At first they fell down a great deal, but then, because Sophie was determined they should succeed, they gradually improved, always remembering to start with the outside feet, and becoming used to a comfortable pattern of stride.

Matthew and Mark even took time off from their training to come and have a look at Sophie and Andrew in double harness.

"Not bad!" they said.

"Good balance."

"Nice rhythm."

"Steady pace."

"Take some beating!"

* * *

Sophie woke on the morning of sports day feeling quite confident that victory would be hers (and Andrew's of course). No other pair of infants could hold a candle to them, she was sure.

To cap it all, it was a lovely day, sunny and warm, and Sophie went happily to school. She did not worry that there was no sign of Andrew. He's late, she thought. But then the teacher called his name at registration and there was no answer!

The secretary put her head round the classroom door.

"Andrew's mother's just rung," she said. "He's got the mumps."

"There's always the infants' egg-and-spoon race," the twins said when Sophie told them the terrible news at playtime.

"I'm not fast enough."

"You don't have to be fast for the egg-and-spoon," said Mark. "You just have to concentrate on the potato."

"What potato?"

"They don't actually use eggs," said Matthew. "And the fast ones always drop their potatoes."

"Just go steady," they said.

Nobody was surprised that afternoon when, between them, the twins won all the lower junior boys' races. Matthew just beat Mark in the sixty metres and Mark just beat Matthew in the hundred metres, and, thanks to the pair of them, their team easily won the relay.

Sophie had no such luck in the infants' races. She tried hard despite her disappointment over

Andrew, but was usually among the last to finish. Worse, however, was to come.

"Now then," said the teacher who was organizing the three-legged race, "everybody stand beside their partners." And she went round tying legs together.

"Sophie," she said at last, "where's your partner?"

"He's got the mumps," said Sophie in a voice of deepest gloom.

"Then we must find you another. Now, who still hasn't got someone to run with?"

"Me, miss," said a voice. "Samantha's gone on holiday."

It was Dawn.

"Yuk!" said Sophie. "I don't want to run with her."

"Don't be silly, Sophie. Come here, Dawn."

63

When all the pairs
were lined up for the race,
it was only too plain that one was
dreadfully unsuited. Lanky Dawn with
her neat blonde ringlets towered over dark stocky
Sophie, who looked, as always, as though she had

just come through a hedge backwards. And it was very apparent that only the length of material binding them together stopped them from putting as much distance as possible between one another.

"Go!" shouted the teacher, and away went the other couples, their arms round each other's shoulders.

Now, all those minutes, hours even, of painstaking practice with poor, fat-necked Andrew were as nothing. Sophie led off with her left foot and Dawn did the same, and they fell in a heap.

Struggling up, they stumbled and shambled behind – off balance, out of step, and hopelessly ill-matched. Time and again they fell, until at last Dawn burst into tears and lay, howling.

Sophie did not approve of crying. She was simply very angry.

"You wimp!" she said
bitterly. "I ought to thump you.
You're mowldy, stupid and
assive, you are," and she
undid the binding,
got to her feet and
stumped off.

*　　*　　*

"Hard luck, Sophie," said Matthew.

"It was that crummy Dawn," said Mark.

"There's still the egg-and-spoon race," said Matthew.

"Concentrate on the potato," said Mark.

"You can do it!" they said.

The potatoes were of all shapes and sizes, and by sheer good luck Sophie was given a nice heavy one that fitted well into the bowl of the spoon. That was a help, no doubt about it, but more important was the fact that Sophie remembered her brothers' advice to go steady.

Several of the infants galloped away at the start of the race, especially the still-snivelling Dawn who was anxious to get as far away from Sophie as she could. And before long potatoes were rolling everywhere on the grass.

Soon all the faster runners were in trouble. The race, it was plain, was between Sophie and Duncan – who was also going along very steadily, possibly because his short legs would carry him no faster.

Neck and neck they plodded on, while the twins yelled encouragement to their sister, and then Duncan tripped and fell, and Sophie came home the winner.

That evening Sophie was sitting in the potting-shed, chatting to Beano as he polished off a carrot, when Tomboy appeared in the doorway. Having made sure that the rabbit was safely shut in his hutch, she came over to be stroked and petted.

"Shall I tell you something, Tomboy?" said Sophie. "Today I won the infants' egg-and-spoon race."

"Yee-oo?" said Tomboy.

"Yes, me. What do you think of that, my dear?" said Sophie.

Her black cat purred very loudly indeed.

Lost and Found

Shortly after sports day, Matthew and Mark went to the seaside on a school camp. Sophie was too young to go. Not that she minded – she was fond of the twins, of course, but they were so noisy, always rushing everywhere and shouting at each other, that it would be nice to have a bit of peace and quiet for one week out of the fifty-two. Besides, she had Tomboy and Beano for company.

*   *   *

"Poor Sophie, she'll be lonely," said her mother.

"She'll miss the boys, I expect," said her father.

"Perhaps," said her mother, "we ought to give her a special treat, to make up for not being able to go to camp?"

"Good idea," said her father, "but what?"

They thought for a minute.

"I know!" said Sophie's father.

"I know what you're going to say!" said Sophie's mother, and then they grinned at one another.

"We sound just like the twins!" they said.

Hanging on Sophie's bedroom walls were four pictures, all drawn by Sophie's mother. One was of a cow called Blossom, one was of two hens named April and May, the third was of a Shetland pony called Shorty and the fourth was of a spotty pig by the name of Measles. These were the animals that would one day belong to Sophie when she was a grown-up lady farmer.

That evening, when her parents came in to say goodnight to her, Sophie was sitting up in bed, underneath her portrait gallery, looking at a picture-book. It was, of course, about a farm. On its cover was a picture of a rather fat farmer and a surprised-looking cow. Instead of sitting on a stool and milking the cow into a pail, the farmer was sitting on the pail and milking her into the upturned stool.

"Look what he's doing!" Sophie's father said, pointing.

"He's forgettable," said Sophie.

"Don't you mean 'forgetful'?" said her mother.

"I've forgotten," said Sophie.

"Well, just remember," her father said, "when

you're grown-up and milking your cows, not to be as absent-minded as that."

"I shall have a milking-machine," said Sophie.

"What, for just one cow?"

"I shall have lots of cows. Blossom will have lots of calves, and then they'll grow up and have calves of their own, and soon I'll have hundreds."

"How would you like to see hundreds of cows?" her mother said.

"All different breeds," said her father.

"And masses of pigs."

"And loads of sheep."

"And horses and ponies."

"And hens and ducks and geese."

"And rabbits?" said Sophie.

"Yes, probably."

"And cats?"

"No. No cats. But every kind of farm animal you can think of, as well as tractors and all sorts of machines. At the Royal Wessex Agricultural Show. Tomorrow. Would you like to go?"

"Yikes!" shouted Sophie. "I shan't sleep a wink!"

"Oh, yes you will," they said. "You have a good night's rest. Sleep tight and mind the fleas don't bite."

They tucked her in, kissed her goodnight and turned off the light. Sophie lay wide awake for what seemed to her like ages. I shall never get to sleep, she said to herself after about ten minutes – I'm so excited about tomorrow.

She began to count sheep jumping through a hole in a hedge. At the fifteenth sheep she gave a tremendous yawn and at the twenty-seventh her eyes closed. Next thing she knew, it was broad daylight.

Sophie sat up and looked at her bedside clock. The little hand pointed to six, the big hand to eight.

"Half-past eight!" she cried. "Mummy and Dad must have overslept. We'll all be late getting to the Agricultural Show!"

She leapt out of bed and ran to her parents' bedroom. Yes, there they were – fast asleep still!

"Wakey, wakey! Rise and shine!" said Sophie.

They raised bleary faces, and Sophie's father peered at his watch.

"What sort of time d'you call this?" he mumbled.

"Half-past eight."

Sophie's father sighed.

"It's the little hand that points to the hour," he said, "and the big hand to the minutes. It's twenty to six."

*   *   *

About five hours later (it seemed to Sophie like five years), they arrived at the Royal Wessex Agricultural Society's showground. Never in her life had Sophie seen so many people – people of all ages, from very old ones being pushed about in wheelchairs to very young ones being pushed about in prams.

"We shall never see any of the animals with all that crowd," she said.

"Oh yes, we will," her mother said. "But don't go wandering off, Sophie. You stay by us."

"We don't want you getting lost," her father said. "Now then, where shall we start? Cattle? Pigs? Sheep?"

"Hot dogs," said Sophie.

"But you've just had breakfast."

"I'm starving."

"It's a very warm day for eating hot dogs."

"Not if you have an ice-cream after," said Sophie.

In the dairy cattle lines they found Friesians and Ayrshires and Shorthorns and Guernseys and beautiful little doe-eyed Jersey cows, one of which, Sophie said, was exactly what Blossom would be like, one day.

Amongst all the hens in the poultry tent there were two sitting side by side – the spitting images of April and May. And as they walked towards the pig lines, along came a girl leading a Shetland pony that was Shorty to the life. All I've got to do now, thought Sophie, is to see a pig just like Measles. But there was such a press of people in the pig lines, almost all of them much taller and wider than Sophie, that she had a job to spot a single pig, let alone a spotty one.

After a bit, she caught a glimpse of some pinky-

white ones, and some black ones, and even some
ginger ones with very long snouts, but nothing that
looked remotely like Measles.

Sophie, though small, was very determined, and
she was not going to give up easily. One minute
she was walking along behind her mother and
father, and the next, catching sight of a white pig
with a dark spot on it, she turned and began to
burrow her way through the crowd to get closer to
its pen.

But when at last she reached it, she was
disappointed to see that it only had two or three
spots. She wriggled her way along to the next pen,
and the next, but the pigs in these again only had a
few spots.

The fourth pen was different. Not that the animal
in it was any spottier, but there was a notice above

it, which Sophie could not read, and in the pen, brushing the pig's bristly back, was a man.

Sophie decided to consult him. She knew that children should not speak to strange men, but she badly needed this one's help, and anyway he looked a nice, kind man. He was fat, with a pink face and a squashy nose and rather big ears. In fact he looked a good deal like the pig that he was grooming.

"Excuse me," Sophie said. "Could you tell me what this notice says?"

The pigman stopped his brushing and looked up.

"It do say 'Gloucester Old Spots', young lady," he replied. "That's the name of the breed, see?"

"Oh," said Sophie. "They don't have many spots, do they?"

"Not nowadays," said the pigman. "'Tidn't the

fashion no more. Time was, thisyer breed was covered in spots."

"Like someone with measles?" Sophie said.

The pigman made a deep grunting noise which, since he was smiling, Sophie took to be a laugh.

"You interested in pigs then, are you, young lady?" he said.

"Yes," said Sophie. "I'm going to be a lady farmer when I grow up."

"Oh ar. And you fancies a pig with a girt lot of spots on, do you?"

"Yes."

"Well, you might be lucky. Some piglets is born with plenty, now and again."

"Thanks," said Sophie. "Goodbye."

"Cheerio," said the pigman.

He looked over Sophie's head and said, "I reckon

she'll make a proper farmer, your little girl will."

Sophie turned round to see a perfectly strange man and woman standing behind her.

"The child is nothing to do with us," the man said.

"Disgraceful," the woman said, "the way some people let little children wander about on their own," and they walked away.

"Well I never!" said the pigman. "Lost your mum and dad in the crowd, have you, young lady?"

Sophie nodded. How shall I ever find them again? she thought. Many children would have cried, but Sophie did not approve of crying.

"Don't you fret," said the pigman. "I'll tell you what to do. See that tent over there with a flag flying over it?"

Sophie nodded again.

"That's the Secretary's tent, that is. You go straight there and tell 'em your name, and they'll put it out on the Tannoy. I'd come with you myself but I can't leave thisyer sow, we'm due in the show-ring in a couple of minutes."

Sophie plodded off towards the Secretary's tent, and when she was half-way there she heard the blare of a loudspeaker.

"Here is an announcement," said a voice. "Will a little girl called Sophie come to the Secretary's tent, where her parents are waiting for her?"

"Well, I'm coming, aren't I?" said Sophie crossly, and then she saw her mother and father standing outside the tent, looking anxiously around. When they caught sight of her, they ran to meet her.

"Oh darling!" her mother cried as she grabbed Sophie and hugged her. "We've been worried stiff!"

"Where on earth did you get to?" her father said.

"I was just having a conservation," Sophie said.

"A conservation?"

"With a nice pigman."

"Don't you mean a 'conversation'?"

"That's what I said. We were talking."

"What about?"

"Pigs, of course. Can I have another hot dog?"

"Oh, Sophie!" they said.

"And another ice-cream."

"Much Too Young"

Sophie was walking Beano round the lawn on a lead.

At one time, before the arrival of the rabbit, she had had the idea of treating Tomboy in a similar fashion. After all, people took their dogs for walks – why not their cats? So she had opened her piggybank and used some of the precious Farm Munny to buy a little collar and lead.

Tomboy had submitted to the fitting of the

collar, but when Sophie attached the lead to it and
said, "Come on, Tomboy! Walkies!" the black cat
had simply lain on her back and batted at the lead
with her forepaws like a kitten playing with a piece
of string. Tugging, Sophie found, only produced
growls and tail-lashings, so she gave up the attempt
at cat-walking. She had left the collar on because
she thought it looked nice – it was a blue one –
until Aunt Al had told her that it was dangerous
for an outdoor cat to wear a collar.

"It might get caught on a twig when Tomboy was
tree-climbing, you see," she had said, "and then
she'd choke herself."

So Sophie had hung up collar and lead in the
potting-shed until such time as she should be
allowed a puppy of her own, something which she
was hopeful would happen one day.

In the meantime, Beano had arrived, and one morning Sophie tried the blue collar on him. It fitted perfectly – it looked rather nice against his snowy fur and he did not seem to object. "And," said Sophie, "one thing's certain – you won't be climbing any trees." So she left it round his neck.

Beano's hutch was positioned low down, merely raised above the floor of the shed by the height of the four bricks it stood on. This had been done partly because Sophie was not tall, but chiefly so that the rabbit could hop out and down when Sophie was cleaning the hutch, and then hop up and back in again easily. The potting-shed door was of course kept shut at these times. Watching him lolloping about on the floor in his new blue collar, Sophie suddenly thought how much he might enjoy a walk on grass.

She clipped the lead on to the collar and opened the door of the shed. For a few moments Beano sat in the doorway, wiffling his nose madly at all the scents of the garden, and then he hopped out, Sophie following.

She soon found that though you may take a dog for a walk, going wherever you wish, that's not the case with a rabbit. The rabbit takes you for the walk and goes wherever it pleases.

But there was no doubt that Beano was greatly enjoying this new experience. He hopped about all over the lawn,

sometimes so quickly that Sophie had to run
to keep up, and now and again he gave a little
buck-jump of excitement. At first he pleased
himself entirely where he went – into the
flower-beds and then into the vegetable patch –
until Sophie hit upon a way, if not to lead him,
at least to steer him roughly in the direction she
wanted. On their next outing she held the lead
in one hand and in the other a Special Rabbit
Controller which she had invented. This was a flat
square of stout cardboard which she had fixed on

to the end of a bamboo cane, and by holding it, for example, on the left side of Beano's face, she forced him to turn right. She had got the idea from remembering how the pigmen at the Royal Wessex Agricultural Show had driven their charges to and from the show-ring by using screens to direct them. (Her nice pigman had, to her delight, won the breed championship with his Gloucester Old Spots sow.) Now, using the Special Rabbit Controller, she could steer the rabbit away from her mother's dahlias or her father's cabbages, and could guide him back into the potting-shed at the end of the outing.

Each day (for by now the summer holidays had arrived) Beano took Sophie for a walk on the grass.

One morning Sophie's father sat on the swing-seat by the edge of the lawn reading the Sunday papers and watching Sophie controlling her rabbit (with difficulty, for Beano was in a contrary mood).

"What you need, Sophie," he said, "is a Labour-saving Device."

"What's that mean?"

"I'll show you," her father said. "I've had an idea that will take all the hard work out of rabbit-exercising."

He got up and went to his workshop at the back of the garage, and came back in a little while with a hammer and a long iron spike which he drove into the lawn.

"Now then," he said, "drop the loop on the end of the lead over the spike, and then Beano can go round and round, so far and no further, and get his exercise and his grazing, and you can put your feet up."

"Daddy," said Sophie, "you're brill."

She sat beside him on the swing-seat and
watched Beano, now safely tethered, nibbling
happily away in the sunshine, and presently
Tomboy came stalking across the lawn, keeping
carefully out of the range of the rabbit, and jumped
up on her lap, purring fit to bust.

My own black cat and my own white rabbit,
thought Sophie. Who could ask for anything more?

"Daddy?" she said. "When
can I have a puppy?"

"Not till
you're old
enough."

"I'm six
this Christmas.
(Sophie's birthday
was on Christmas Day.)

"Much too young."

"Seven?"

"No."

"Eight then?"

"Possibly."

Sophie rubbed the tip of her nose.

"Matthew and Mark are eight," she said.

"So?"

"So they're old enough to have a puppy.
Only of course they'll need two – one each."

Her father laid down his newspaper.

"I can read you like a book, madam," he said. "You know the twins aren't all that interested in animals, so if they were allowed a puppy (and you can forget about two, right now), you'd take it over. That was what you were thinking, wasn't it?"

Sophie did not approve of telling lies so she said, "Yes."

"You've got your own black cat and your own rabbit."

"Yes."

"Well then."

Sophie sat silent on the swing-seat for some little time, while her father rocked it gently with one foot as he read his paper, and Tomboy purred, and Beano grazed.

Then she said, "Andrew's only five like me and

he's got three dogs."

"Andrew?"

"Yes. You know. Where I fell in the cowpat."

"Oh, the farmer's son."

"Yes. He's got three."

"Fancy."

"Two sheepdogs and a terrier called Lucy."

"But they aren't his dogs, are they? They're his father's dogs."

"Yes. But he's lucky, Andrew is, all the same."

There was another silence, broken only by the purr of the cat and a little squeaking noise as the seat swung to and fro.

"Isn't he?" said Sophie.

"Isn't who what?"

"Andrew. Lucky."

"Mm."

Silence again for a moment. Tomboy jumped down and walked away. Beano sat up and scratched his ear. The seat squeaked.

"She's going to have babies, sometime later on this year, Andrew told me," said Sophie.

"Who is?"

"Lucy."

Sophie's father sighed and folded his newspaper.

"Sophie love," he said, "I've read the same sentence about five times. How about going and asking Mum if she'd put the kettle on? I wouldn't mind a mug of coffee."

And I wouldn't mind one of Lucy's puppies when she has them, thought Sophie as she plodded off. It's not fair. Fancy having to wait till I'm eight. That's nearly two and a half years. And then they'll probably still say "No". I wish I was grown up.

"Mum," she said, when she had given the message. "When you were a child, did you have a dog of your very own?"

"Yes, I did, Sophie. When Granpa and Granny thought I was responsible enough to look after it properly – to feed it and groom it and train it and exercise it. 'You shall have a puppy of your own,' they said, 'once you're old enough.'"

"And how old was that?"

"Twelve."

That evening, when the children were all in bed, Sophie's father said to his wife, "Did you have a dog of your own when you were a child?"

"How odd!" she replied. "Sophie asked me that, this morning."

"Really?"

"Yes, and I told her I did, but not till I was twelve. They didn't think I was old enough till then."

"Ah. What sort was it?"

"A little terrier."

"Funny," said Sophie's father. "I wasn't allowed a dog of my own when I was a boy, but I always wanted a little terrier."

"Do you still?"

Sophie's father laughed. "I'm certainly old enough now," he said.

Sophie's mother laughed. "Me too," she said.

One Final
Present

Before you could look round, it seemed to Sophie, those sunny summer holidays were over and the children were going back to school.

Matthew and Mark had nearly always gone off to play football with their friends, so Sophie had really only seen them at mealtimes.

It was much the same at school, except that now it was proper football with a proper pitch and goalposts.

One day
the twins
came home
in a state
of high
excitement.

"What's
up with you
two?" their
mother said.
"Scored a goal
each, have you?"

"No, Mum," said Mark. "It's the school concert."

"You know," said Matthew. "At the end of this term."

"We've got parts in the juniors' play!" they said.

"I wish I could be in a play," said Sophie.

"You might be," said Matthew.

"The infants do one too, you know," said Mark.

"Who d'you think we're going to be, Mum?" said Matthew.

"Have a guess," said Mark.

"I don't even know what the play is," said their mother. "You'll have to tell me that first."

"It's all different bits out of *Alice in Wonderland*," said Mark.

"And *Alice through the Looking-glass*," said Matthew.

"All put together," they said.

"You're a crazy couple," said their mother. "I should think you're going to be the Mad Hatter and the March Hare."

"No!" they shouted.

"I'm Tweedledum!" said Matthew.

"And I'm Tweedledee!" said Mark.

"And we're going to be all stuffed out with cushions …"

"… to make us look fat …"

"… and have a great battle …"

"…with toy swords!"

"Football and fighting!" said Sophie scornfully when the twins had run whooping away. "That's all boys think about."

"Perhaps you'll get a nice part in the infants' play," her mother said.

The very next day, as it happened, Sophie's teacher said to her class, "Now, after the end of this term, there's a very special day to look forward to. Who can tell me what it is called?"

A forest of hands shot up.

"Well, Dawn?"

"It's Christmas Day."

"And what's special about Christmas Day? Andrew?"

"You get lots of presents."

"That's not what I meant. Yes, Duncan?"

"You get a lot to eat."

"No, no," said the teacher. "Never mind about presents or food. Christmas Day is special because that's when we celebrate a very important birthday. And whose birthday is that?"

"Mine," said Sophie.

The teacher looked hard at Sophie. Then she opened her register and ran a finger down the class list of dates of birth.

Then she said, "Yes, Sophie, I remember now that your birthday is on Christmas Day. But I'm talking

about a baby who was born nearly two thousand years ago, in Bethlehem."

Dawn's long skinny arm was raised.

"Yes, Dawn?"

"Jesus."

"Yes, that's right, good girl. Now you all remember the story of Jesus's birth, don't you? He was born in a stable, wasn't He?"

"Yes."

"Why?"

"They were full up in the pub," said Sophie.

"I don't think that's the right word to use, Sophie," said the teacher. "It was simply an inn where travellers rested. But yes, there was no room at the inn, so the baby was born in the stable and laid in a manger. What's a manger, someone? Andrew?"

"It's like a wooden trough," said Andrew. "You put hay in it. But we don't."

"Why not?"

"We make silage."

"Oh. I see. Anyway, this is what I want to tell you all. At the end of this term we shall have the school concert, and this class is going to act its own little play, all about the birth of Jesus. There'll be Mary and Joseph and the Wise Men and the shepherds and the innkeeper and … now who have I forgotten?"

"The ox and the ass," said Sophie. "That could be me and Andrew, couldn't it?"

"No, Sophie, the animals will just be painted on the scenery. Now who will be the most important person in the whole play?"

"Baby Jesus!" they all chorused.

"Please, miss," said Duncan. "Can I be Baby Jesus?"

"He's small enough," said Sophie drily.

"No, no, Duncan, the baby will be represented by a doll. I couldn't have a live baby on the stage."

"You wouldn't have time," said Sophie.

"It takes nine months, like a cow," said Andrew.

Possibly these last two remarks had something to do with the fact that, when the leading parts in the play were allotted, Sophie and Andrew were passed over.

"Don't worry," said the teacher to those without starring roles. "You'll all be dressing up and singing 'Once in Royal David's City'."

"I'm in the infants' play," said Sophie that evening.

"Oh good," said her father. "Who else in your class is in it?"

"Everyone."

"Oh. What's it about?"

"It's an activity play."

"Don't you mean a 'nativity' play?"

"No, it's about Baby Jesus being born."

"Are you Mary?" said Mark.

"No."

"Who is?" said Matthew.

"Dawn," said Sophie.

"Yuk!" they said.

"Well, you can't be Joseph …"

"… or a Wise Man …"

"… or a shepherd …"

"… or the innkeeper …"

"… because they'll all be boys …"

"…so who are you?"

"I'm a crowd," said Sophie.

"Well, at least you won't have any words to learn, then," her mother said.

"Except rhubarb, rhubarb, rhubarb," said her father.

"Why rhubarb?"

"That's what everyone says in crowd scenes."

Later, when the infant class had the first rehearsal of their Christmas play, Sophie and Andrew and the rest of the extras stood at the back of the stage, while Joseph and Mary and the innkeeper and the Wise Men and the shepherds were pushed and pulled into their proper places.

Mary, Dawn that is, had brought in to school a bald baby doll of her own, and had beforehand been preparing to wrap its bare pink body in swaddling clothes, when Sophie had chanced by.

"That's no good," she said.

"Why not?" said Dawn.

"You blind?" said Sophie. "It's a girl."

But now Mary sat nursing the baby,

Joseph standing proudly at her side, and on came
the shepherds and the Wise Men bearing their gifts
which they presented. But all the time no one
said anything, not a word.

Sophie looked about at all the others in the
crowd, but they too were silent. Sillies, she thought,
they don't know what to say. But I do, and loudly
she cried, "Rhubarb, rhubarb, rhubarb!"

"Anybody would think rhubarb was a rude word,"
said Sophie afterwards to an audience of two,
Tomboy and Beano.

"Nee-o," said Tomboy.

"Well, the teacher got ever so mad with me, and
I was only doing what Dad said. She's mowldy,
stupid and assive, that's what she is."

*   *   *

Not long after the half-term break, Andrew said to Sophie, "Lucy's got puppies."

"How many?" said Sophie.

"Six."

"Yikes!"

"You can come and see them if you like."

Sophie hesitated. She longed to see the puppies, but she knew it would be awful because she would want one of them so much.

Unwittingly, Andrew made matters worse.

"You could have one when they're old enough," he said.

"No," said Sophie. "They won't let me. Not till I'm eight."

"Well, d'you want to see them or not? Make your mind up."

Sophie made it up.

"OK," she said. "I'd better come to tea. You ask your mummy to ask my mummy if I can."

Sophie never forgot the first time she set eyes on that litter of six fat little terrier puppies. They were a fortnight old, their eyes not long opened, and they were just beginning to stumble about on their short legs.

All puppies are delightful creatures, especially to someone who is determined to become a lady farmer.

Lucy, the mother, was a smooth-haired small white terrier with some black patches.

"But the father of the pups," said Andrew's father, "was brown and white, so most of these have got some brown on them too. Which one do you like best, Sophie?"

Sophie rubbed the tip of her nose.

"That one," she said, and she pointed to a puppy that was all white except for a black patch over his right eye. "I just wish I could have him."

"Well, I'm going to sell the lot when they're old enough," said the farmer. "You'd better ask your mum and dad."

"They won't let me," said Sophie. "They say I'm too young."

"And how old are you?"

"I'll be six on Christmas Day."

"Will you indeed?" said Andrew's father. "Well, they're right. You are too young to have a dog of your own, same as Andrew here. Haven't your family a dog at all?"

"No."

"No animals?"

"I've got a cat and a rabbit," Sophie said.

"Ah well, you aren't doing too badly then. I dare say they'll get a dog one day. Come on then, Lucy – in you go with your pups. And Andrew and Sophie – it's time for tea."

With one last backward look at the white puppy with the black patch over his right eye, Sophie plodded off. I don't want to see them again, she said to herself. If Andrew asks me to tea before they're all sold, I shan't go. I couldn't bear it.

In fact, Andrew did not ask her again as November and the early part of December sped by, and soon the school concert was upon them.

Sophie's mother and father came with all the other parents to watch.

The nativity play went pretty well except that one of the Wise Men was silly enough to drop his gift. Sophie, wrapped in a red-checked gingham tablecloth and positioned at the rear of the crowd, remained silent, only mouthing "Rhubarb" when she caught her parents' eyes.

As for Tweedledum, he had the most tremendous fight with Tweedledee for stealing his nice new rattle, and, all in all, the concert was a great success.

Hardly was it over, it seemed to Sophie, than it was Christmas Eve, the eve of her sixth birthday.

Christmas Day began as usual – the stockings, then breakfast, then the giving out of the presents, all stacked beneath the Christmas tree. Just before they started on that, the phone rang and it was Aunt Al, to wish them the compliments of the season.

When it was Sophie's turn to speak, she said, "How's Ollie?"

"He's fine," said Aunt Al. "He's grown. He's going to be the biggest cat in the Highlands, I should think."

"As big as a Scottish Wild Cat?"

"Shouldn't wonder. Have you had any good presents?"

"We haven't opened them yet."

"Hope you get a nice surprise," said Aunt Al.

As always, the presents were opened one at a time, youngest first. One for Sophie, then one for Mark, then Matthew, then Mummy, then Dad, and finally a birthday present for Sophie before she began again on her next Christmas one.

But this year, when all the presents had been undone and there was nothing left under the tree, Sophie's father said, "Now everybody stay put and play with your presents. I shan't be more than quarter of an hour," and out he went.

They heard the car start up.

"Where's Dad gone, Mum?" said Matthew.

"To fetch something."

"What is it?" said Mark.

"One final present."

"Who's it for?" said Sophie.

"All of us."

"For all of us?" said the three children with one voice.

"Yes. It's for Daddy and it's for me and it's for Matthew and it's for Mark and it's for Sophie."

The twins shook their heads.

"I don't get it," said Mark.

"Me neither," said Matthew.

As for Sophie, she suddenly remembered that in all the excitement she had fed neither Tomboy nor Beano, and she went off to give each a special Christmas breakfast.

No sooner was she back in the sitting-room with the others than they all heard the car returning.

"Sit still," their mother said. "Don't move."

The door opened, and in walked their father, carrying something in his arms.

When Sophie saw what it was, for once in her life she did not shout "Yikes!" because her throat had suddenly tightened up so that she could not have got the sound out. And for once, though she did not approve of crying, her eyes filled with tears.

They were tears of happiness, at the sight of the puppy that was all white except for a black patch over his right eye.

THE END

Dick King-Smith (1922–2011), a former dairy farmer, is one of the world's favourite children's book authors. He won the Guardian Fiction Prize for *The Sheep-Pig* (later filmed as *Babe*), was named Children's Book Author of the Year in 1991 and won the 1995 Children's Book Award for *Harriet's Hare*. His titles for Walker include the Sophie books, *Aristotle*, *Lady Lollipop* and its sequel, *Clever Lollipop*.

David Parkins has illustrated a number of children's books, including the picture books *Prowlpuss* (shortlisted for the 1994 Kurt Maschler Award, and the 1995 Smarties Book Prize) and *Webster J. Duck*, written by Hans Christian Andersen Award-winner Martin Waddell. David was born in Brighton but now lives in Canada.

Yikes! There are six books about Sophie altogether:

 Sophie's Snail

 Sophie's Tom

 Sophie Hits Six

 Sophie in the Saddle

 Sophie Is Seven

 Sophie's Lucky